JEEPERS CREEPERS

All inquiries should be addressed to:
Barron's Educational Series, Inc.
250 Wireless Boulevard
Hauppauge, NY 11788

International Standard Book Number 0-8120-1841-9

Library of Congress Catalog Card Number 93-43091

Library of Congress Cataloging-in-Publication Data

Foster, Kelli C.
    Jeepers creepers / by Foster & Erickson : illustrations by
Kerri Gifford.
        p. cm.— (Get ready—get set—read!)
    Summary: A little girl falls asleep counting sheep and dreams
of helping Little Bo Peep.
    ISBN 0-8120-1841-9
    1. Stories in rhyme. (1. Sleep—Fiction. 2. Sheep—Fiction.)
I. Erickson, Gina Clegg. II. Gifford, Kerri, ill. III. Title.
IV. Series: Erickson, Gina Clegg. Get ready—get set—read!
PZ8.3.F813Je 1994
(E)—dc20
                                                        93-43091
                                                        CIP
                                                        AC

PRINTED IN HONG KONG
567   9927   98765432

GET READY...GET SET...READ!

JEEPERS CREEPERS

by
Foster & Erickson

Illustrations by
Kerri Gifford

FOREST HOUSE ®
School & Library Edition

Jeepers, creepers!
I'm not sleepy.
I cannot go to sleep.

I think I need to
count some sheep.

Now let's see,
one, two, three,

and one more,
that makes four…

Then without a peep
she went to sleep.

Don't weep, Little Bo-Peep.
Stay here and we will
find your sheep.

I think I know
where the sheep would go.
In there!

This is creepy.
But we must keep
going to find the sheep.

Jeepers, creepers!
This is deep and getting deeper

Hold on!
We must find the sheep.

Up there!
This is steep and
getting steeper.

Keep going!
We must find the sheep.

Jeepers, creepers!
We found the sheep.

Now let's go
and get Bo-Peep.

"Thanks for finding my sheep.
Now we all can get some sleep

The End

The EEP Word Family

Bo-Peep
creepers
creepy
deep
deeper
jeepers
peep
sheep
sleep
sleepy
steep
steeper
weep

Sight Words

now
one
two
four
some
stay
count
would
thanks

Dear Parents and Educators:

Welcome to *Get Ready...Get Set...Read!*

We've created these books to introduce children to the magic of reading.

Each story in the series is built around one or two word families. For example, *A Mop for Pop* uses the OP word family. Letters and letter blends are added to OP to form words such as TOP, LOP, and STOP. As you can see, once children are able to read OP, it is a simple task for them to read the entire word family. In addition to word families, we have used a limited number of "sight words." These are words found to occur with high frequency in the books your child will soon be reading. Being able to identify sight words greatly increases reading skill.

You might find the steps outlined on the facing page useful in guiding your work with your begining reader.

We had great fun creating these books, and great pleasure sharing them with our children. We hope *Get Ready...Get Set...Read!* helps make this first step in reading fun for you and your new reader.

Kelli C. Foster, PhD
Educational Psychologist

Gina Clegg Erickson, MA
Reading Specialist

Guidelines for Using *Get Ready...Get Set...Read!*

Step 1.   Read the story to your child.

Step 2.   Have your child read the Word Family list aloud
           several times.

Step 3.   Invent new words for the list. Print each new
           combination for your child to read. Remember,
           nonsense words can be used (*dat, kat, gat*).

Step 4.   Read the story *with* your child. He or she reads
           all of the Word Family words; you read the rest.

Step 5.   Have your child read the Sight Word list aloud
           several times.

Step 6.   Read the story *with* your child again. This time
           he or she reads the words from both lists; you
           read the rest.

Step 7.   Your child reads the entire book to you!

Titles in the

Series:

SET 1

Find Nat
The Sled Surprise
Sometimes I Wish
A Mop for Pop
The Bug Club
BRING-IT-ALL-TOGETHER BOOKS
What a Day for Flying!
Bat's Surprise

SET 2

The Tan Can
The Best Pets Yet
Pip and Kip
Frog Knows Best
Bub and Chub
BRING-IT-ALL-TOGETHER BOOKS
Where Is the Treasure?
What a Trip!

SET 3

Jake and the Snake
Jeepers Creepers
Two Fine Swine
What Rose Does Not Know
Pink and Blue
BRING-IT-ALL-TOGETHER BOOKS
The Pancake Day
Hide and Seek*

SET 4

Whiptail of Blackshale Trail
Colleen and the Bean*
Dwight and the Trilobite
The Old Man at the Moat
By the Light of the Moon
BRING-IT-ALL-TOGETHER BOOKS
Night Light*
The Crossing*

SET 5

Tall and Small
Bounder's Sound*
How to Catch a Butterfly*
Ludlow Grows Up*
Matthew's Brew
BRING-IT-ALL-TOGETHER BOOKS
Snow in July*
Let's Play Ball*

* Forthcoming title